Some of my ge[...]

'Will make you laugh out loud, cringe and snigger, all at the same time'
—LoveReading4Kids

'WHAT'S NOT TO LOVE?' —Sun

'Very funny and cheeky'
—Booktictac, Guardian Online Review

Waterstones **Children's Book Prize Shortlistee!**

'I LAUGHED SO MUCH, I THOUGHT THAT I WAS GOING TO BURST!'
Finbar, aged 9

'The review of the eight year old boy in our house...
"Can I keep it to give to a friend?"
Best recommendation you can get' —Observer

'HUGELY ENJOYABLE, SURREAL CHAOS'
—Guardian

I am not a Loser
The Roald Dahl
FUNNY PRIZE
WINNER 2013

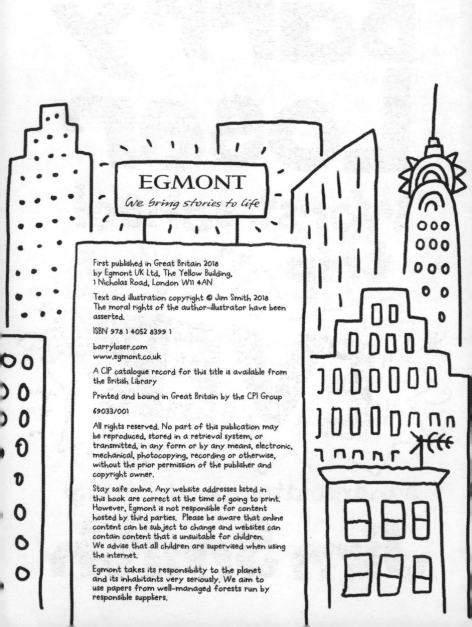

EGMONT
We bring stories to life

First published in Great Britain 2018
by Egmont UK Ltd, The Yellow Building,
1 Nicholas Road, London W11 4AN

Text and illustration copyright © Jim Smith 2018
The moral rights of the author-illustrator have been
asserted.

ISBN 978 1 4052 8399 1

barryloser.com
www.egmont.co.uk

A CIP catalogue record for this title is available from
the British Library

Printed and bound in Great Britain by the CPI Group

69033/001

Barry Loser

Worst school trip

EVER

Banana later slipped on by

Jim Smith

How it started

My annoying little brother, Desmond Loser the Second, always gets everything his own way.

being on first page for example

Like the other morning when me, him, my mum and dad were all sitting round the kitchen table before school.

bit tired →

really tired ↓

pretty tired ↑

wide awake ←

I was happily flipping through my
Future Ratboy Fan Club Magazine,
imagining I was a superhero like him,
when Des opened his mouth.

'Me want Bazzy's brekkie!' he wailed,
reaching for my bowl of cereal.

'But we're eating the same thing, Des,' I said in my older brother voice. 'I've got a bowl of Crazy Caterpillars and so have you!'

identikeel

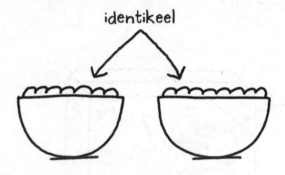

Crazy Caterpillars are the keelest cereal in the whole wide world amen.

They first popped up in an episode of **Future Ratboy**, my favourite TV show. Then one day Feeko's Supermarket started selling them in real life, which made me wee my pants with excitement when I found out.

'Just swap bowls with him, Barry,' said my dad, pressing the button on his brand new coffee machine, which started to whir.

really excited

coffee machine's view

'But you never used to give in to me like that when I was little,' I said, switching my bowl with Desmond's in super slow motion.

arm stretches really far

'I had more energy when there was only one of you,' chuckled my dad, taking a sip of his disgusting drink.

I leaned over and switched the radio on.

Goooooood morrrrrrning Mogden!

screeched a voice out of the speaker.

A song by my dad's favourite band,
Frankie Teacup and the Saucers,
started to play and my dad got up
and wiggled his bum to the music.

'Me no want moosik!'

shouted Desmond.

'Say **PLEASE**, Desmond,' I said, because that's what my mum and dad had taught me to say.

'Just turn the music off would you, Barry?' sighed my mum. 'I was up with Des all blooming night and I can't take any more of his whining.'

'What?!' I said, clicking off the radio. 'But he didn't even say blooming please!'

'Don't say blooming, Barry,' said my mum.

'But you did!' I said.

'I'm a grown-up,' said my mum.

'So am I!' I cried.

'It's not fair,' I whimpered. 'Desmond always gets everything his way!'

My dad chuckled. 'Aren't you off to Hokum City with school this morning, Barry?' he asked.

'Ooh that's right, your big brother's going on a very exciting trip today, Des!' said my mum. 'His teacher, Miss Spivak, got a new boyfriend who works at a big flashy TV studio in Hokum City and he's organised for Barry's class to see an exhibition about the history of television!'

I looked at Des, a string of drool
dangling out of his mouth with a
half-chomped Crazy Caterpillar
hanging off the end of it.

'Urgh, an exhibition about the history of telly,' I groaned. 'Sounds comperleeterly boring to me.'

loserish old TV

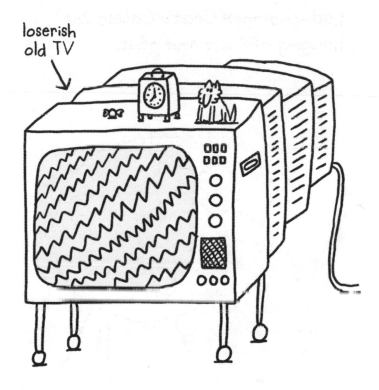

'Don't be a grump Barry,' said my dad. 'It'll be smashing!'

I carried on flipping through my magazine, imagining myself as a giant Barry robot stomping through the streets of Hokum City, smashing up cars and buildings.

real me inside

And that's when it happened.

There, in the background of a photo on page twenty-one of my Future Ratboy Fan Club Magazine, was the answer to my dreamypoos.

GASP!

hey, page twenty-one! ⟶

'Oops, late for work!' said my dad, slurping the rest of his coffee. He kissed us all on the ends of our noses and headed off to his boring job.

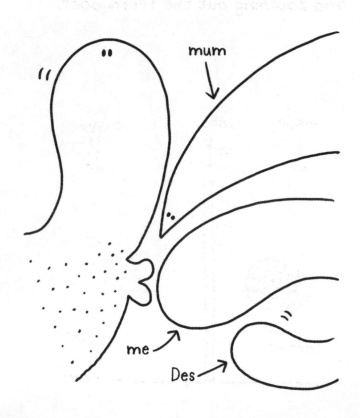

I stood up and stuffed my magazine into my rucksack. 'Mum, Des, I think I might have just had the most brilliant and amazekeel idea ever!' I said, doing an excitement blowoff and zooming out the front door.

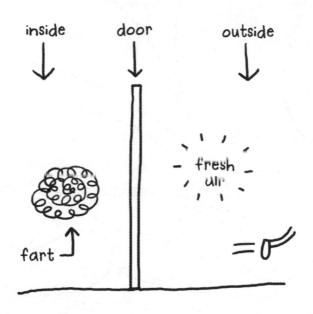

inside   door   outside

fart

fresh air

After that

'This is gonna be the keelest day ever!' I said nine hundred and ninety-nine seconds later. I was walking to school with my best friends - Bunky, and Nancy Verkenwerken.

I was in a much better mood now, partly because I'd got away from Des, but also because I was back where I belonged: being the leader of the Keel Gang.

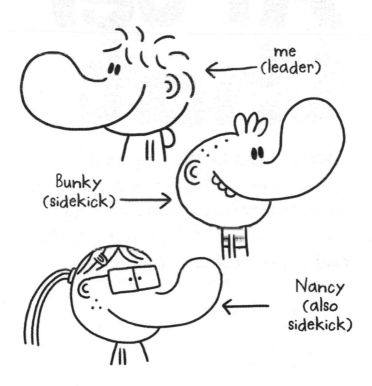

me
(leader)

Bunky
(sidekick) →

Nancy
(also
sidekick)

'But I thought we said that the history of telly exhibition sounded comperleeterly boring?' said Bunky, looking all upset that I'd changed my mind since our phonekeel last night.

'I think it'll be interesting,' said Nancy, pushing her glasses up her nose. 'Plus I can't wait to see all the skyscrapers in Hokum City!'

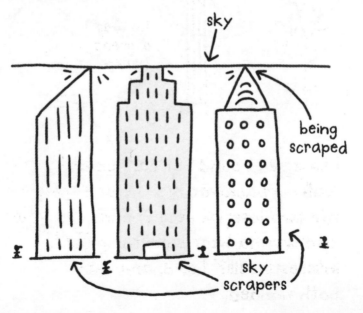

sky

being scraped

sky scrapers

I smiled at Nancy, letting her have her turn to talk. That's what it's like being the leader of a gang - you've got to make sure everyone's happy.

he was a great person

I twizzled round but carried on walking backwards so I was facing my two loserish best friends. 'Do you two wanna hear something REALLY interestikeels?' I said, and they both nodded.

Bin Bazzy

We turned the corner and I tripped, tap-dancing backwards and landing bum-first inside a rubbish bin. Which sounds loserish, but is actukeely pretty keel.

TRIP!

'Who do you think you are - **Future Ratboy**?' sniggled Bunky, and I gave him a mini-salute, because in the **Future Ratboy** TV show, Ratboy gets zapped to the future inside his family's bin.

Future Ratboy

his sidekick Not Bird

'Barry babes, that is NOT a good look for you!' snortled a familikeelsly annoying voice, and I looked over to see Sharonella from my class at school.

Shazza

I plopped my bum out of the bin like a cork and gave it a little pat, just to let it know everything was okay.

'That reminds me Shazza,' I said, which is what I say when I want to change the subject. 'I was just about to tell Bunky and Nancy something comperleeterly amazekeels.'

But then...

"Ello 'ello 'ello, who have we got 'ere then?' said ANOTHER annoying familikeels voice. This time I didn't have to look to know whose it was.

'Mornkeels Dazza,' said Sharonella, as Darren Darrenofski - the crocodile-faced little Fronkle monster from our class - wobbled up, carrying a can of Fronkle. 'We were just talking about the big day trip!'

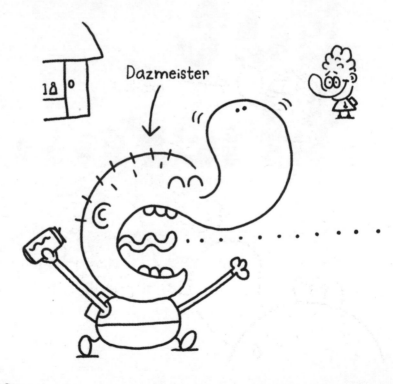

Dazmeister

Darren did a Fronkle burp and blew it in my face. 'Hokum City here we come!' he snuffled. 'Wish we were going to Fronkle World instead of this rubbish history of telly exhibition though.'

really excited

'Can everyone please stop talking and listen to me?' I said, stomping my foot on the pavement, and they all looked at me, which was a start at least.

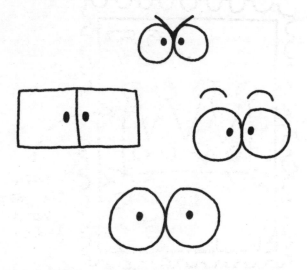

'Oh my days, you make me LARF Barry Loser!' cackled Shazza. 'Who do you think you are, the king of Mogden or something?'

'No,' I said, even though I do sort of think if there was ever going to be a king of Mogden it probably should be me.

hard to get hood over

'Go on then Barry, let's hear your idea,' said Nancy, and I was just about to open my mouth to tell them it when Bunky's opened first.

'Hey look!' he cried, pointing up the road, and I spotted a big fat bus sitting outside our school, waiting to take us to Hokum City.

Millions more seconds later

'Can I PER-LEASE tell you my amazekeel news now?' I said, once we'd all run up the street and got on the scratched-up old bus.

'If you have to,' said Shazza, as the bus's exhaust pipe did a blowoff and we finally started our journey to Hokum City.

All five of us – me, Bunky, Nancy, Darren and Sharonella – were sitting on the back seat, which everyone knows is where the keel people sit.

'Well,' I said, and they all leaned in. 'It just so happens I know a little fact about the TV studio we're going to!'

'What is it, Barry?' burped Darren. 'Not that I care.'

I stared out of the window, letting my loserish friends wait for their leader to speak.

Even in the bright morning sun the shops on Mogden High Street looked comperleeterly loserish and grey compared to the glistening skyscrapers we were about to see in Hokum City.

Miss Spivak counting my head →

'Are any of you lot members of the
Future Ratboy Fan Club?' I asked.

Darren and Sharon shook their
heads. 'I'm Chairman of the Fronkle
Appreciation Society though,'
grinned Darren.

'How many members has it got?'
asked Nancy.

'Just the one,' said Darren, pulling
a shiny new can out of his bag and
cracking it open.

'Bunky?' I said, raising my eyebrows.

'Errr, I forgot to renew my membership,' said Bunky, looking all guilty.

Miss Spivak counting again

'Shame on you, Nigel Zuckerberg,' I said, which is Bunky's real name. He comperleeterly hates it and I only use it when he's been an extremely naughty doggy. 'Give me a quadruple-reverse, upside-down salute - on the double!'

'You two are weird,' burped Darren, watching Bunky do his salute.

'Nancy,' I said. 'How about you?'

'I LIKE Future Ratboy,' she said. 'But not THAT much.'

'Fair enoughkeels,' I said, pulling the **Future Ratboy** Fan Club Magazine out of my rucksack. 'Now, are you ready to hear something that'll blow your tiny little minds?

Michael J Socks

'I shouldn't really be telling you this, seeing as you're not members of the fan club,' I said.

'Just get on with it, Bazza,' snored Sharonella, and I flipped my magazine to page twenty-one, which had a photo of Michael J Socks on it.

Michael J Socks is the amazekeel actor who plays **Future Ratboy** on TV. He's a bit older than me and is comperleeterly rich and famous.

I held my magazine open to the photo of him relaxing on the set of **Future Ratboy**. He was wearing sunglasses and holding a can of passion fruit flavour Fronkle.

me, not Spivak

'Passion Fruit Fronkle?' cried Darren, splurting regular flavour Fronkle all over the back of the seat in front of him. 'Why didn't anyone tell me about this?'

'Ooh, isn't he dishy!' cooed Shazza all grannyishly, leaning over and giving the photo of Michael J Socks a great big sloppy smooch. 'Love ya, Mikey!'

Shazza's Mikey eyes

'Eww,' said Nancy, as I wiped my magazine dry with a bit of Bunky's T-shirt. 'That's gross, Shazza!'

'Not your type, eh Nance?' said Shazza. 'Prefer a bit of a bad boy, do ya?'

A pointy-nosed face popped up over the top of the seat in front of Darren. 'Somebody mention me?' smiled Gordon Smugly, the smug, ugly Gordon from our class at school.

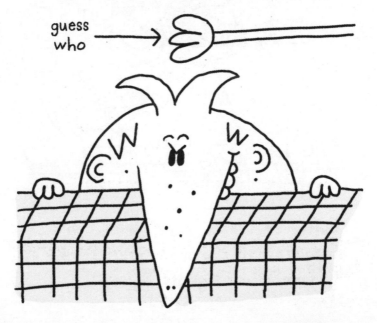

guess who →

'I said BAD, Smugly, not SAD,' said Shazza. I stomped my foot on the ground, except my foot wasn't long enough to reach the floor from my seat, so it just sort of swung a bit.

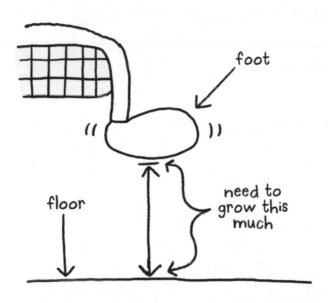

foot

floor

need to grow this much

'For crying out keel, would you please let me talk!' I boomed.

The blooming moustache

'Silence, for King Loser is about to speak!' sniggled Sharonella.

'Thank you Shazzoid,' I said, although I wasn't sure why she was sniggling. I held the photo of Michael J Socks up again. 'Now, can anyone see anything interestikeels in this photo?'

They all peered at the picture. 'Ooh, I know!' blurted Bunky, looking like he was holding in an excitement blowoff. 'Michael J Socks is growing a moustache!'

'Eh?' I said, zooming my eyes in on Michael J Socks's upper lip.

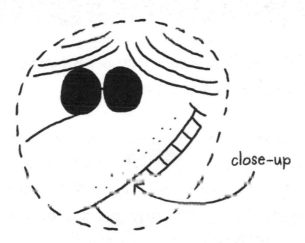

close-up

Bunky was right. Just under his nose was a row of tiny dots, just like the ones my dad gets half an hour after he's shaved.

Sharonella looked at me and fluttered her eyelashes. 'Reckon you'd look good with a moustache, Bazzy,' she smiled.

me with moustache

'Forget about the blooming moustache!' I cried, waggling my fingers at the top bit of the photo. 'What about BEHIND Michael J Socks?'

All eight of their eyeballs zoomed
in on the background of the photo,
which was the set of **Future Ratboy**.
Wooden cut-outs of futuristikeel
skyscrapers zigzagged up into the
sky. Just behind them, ever-so-
slighterly blurry, was a sign.

even
closer-up

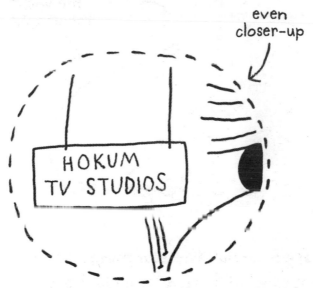

'Hokum TV Studios,' said Sharonella,
reading what it said. 'Hey, isn't that
the place we're off to today?'

'Yep,' I smiled. '**Future Ratboy** is filmed in the same place we're going!'

I breathed out, feeling relieved that I'd finally managed to tell my loserish friends what I'd been holding in since my annoying breakfast with Des.

Crazy Caterpillar flavour

'Trouble is though, Barry,' said Bunky, 'we're going to that boring old history of telly exhibition instead.'

THE BLACK AND
WHITE YEARS

'Bunky, Bunky, Bunky,' I said. 'All we have to do is sneak out of the exhibition and onto the Future RatBoy oot!'

'How are we going to do that, though?' asked Gordon, popping his head over his seat again, chomping on a banana.

I ignored Gordon and turned to
Bunky and Nancy. I was sort of
facing Darren and Sharonella too,
not that I exackerly wanted them
in on the plan.

'What I was thinking was this . . .'
I said, and I started to explain
my idea.

The poo poo plan

'Hmm, I'm not sure Miss Spivak will buy that,' said Nancy, once I'd explained my plan, which was this:

Halfway through the tour of the history of telly exhibition, we all pretend we really really need poos and go off to the toilets, but sneak onto the **Future Ratboy** set instead.

'What's wrong with it?' I said.
'It's geniuskeels!'

'It's just not believable that so many people would need a poo at the exact same time,' said Nancy.

all serious about it

'Yeah that idea's rubbish, Barold!' said
Gordon, finishing off his banana and
reaching over to plonk the skin
carefully on top of my hairdo.

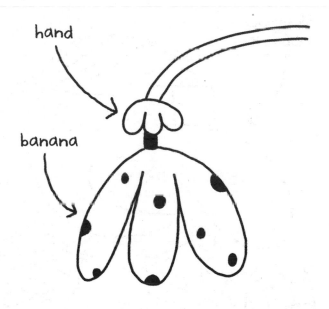

hand

banana

I shook the banana skin off my head
and looked out of the bus window.
Far in the hazy distance, the tip of
the world famous Milk Carton Tower
was peeking over the horizon.

Milk Carton
Tower

Wine Bottle
Building

Orange Juice
Mansions

'Hey, that's Hokum City!' cried Bunky,
and deep inside my tummy I felt a
chomped-up Crazy Caterpillar
transform into an excited butterfly.

Hokum City

'Come on then Nance, what's your plan for sneaking off?' asked Sharonella, as the bus chugged across a ginormous bridge into Hokum City.

'I don't have one,' said Nancy.

'Think Nancy, THINK!' said Bunky.
'Don't you want to meet **Future Ratboy?**'

Nancy rolled her eyes. 'You wouldn't be meeting **Future Ratboy,**' she said. 'You'd be meeting *Michael J Socks.*'

'Ooh, just imagine!' cooed Sharonella. 'How's my hair look?' she said, peering past me at her reflection in the window.

Darren crumpled his empty can of Regular Fronkle and balanced it on top of Stuart Shmendrix's head, which was sitting on top of Stuart Shmendrix's body, which was sitting next to the whole of Gordon Smugly.

perfect head for putting can on

Gordon's smug, ugly face popped back up. 'Who dares make a fool out of my new best friend Stuart Shmendrix?' he snapped.

'It was Barry,' smiled Darren, turning to Nancy. 'Go on Nance, come up with one of your clever little ideas for us!'

'Whoa, whoa, whoa,' I said. 'I'm the one who comes up with the genius plans around here, Darrenofski!'

Nancy glanced at me like I was an idiot, which I'm comperleeterly not. 'I suppose the idea of you all needing to go to the toilet at the same time isn't too bad,' she said. 'You just need to swap the poo bit for something more convincing.'

'Wee?' said Bunky.

silly doggy

'How about if we were all feeling a bit dodgy from the bus journey?' said Sharonella, looking down the aisle at Fay Snoggles, who was sitting at the front next to Miss Spivak because she always gets travel sick.

Nancy itched her glasses, which was weird.

'how do glasses itch?'

'Not bad, Shazza,' she said. 'Not bad at all . . .'

And then Nancy's eyes lit up like the brain behind them had just had an amazekeel idea.

'What is it, Nancy?' I said, as the bus did a blowoff and shuddered to a stop outside Hokum TV Studios.

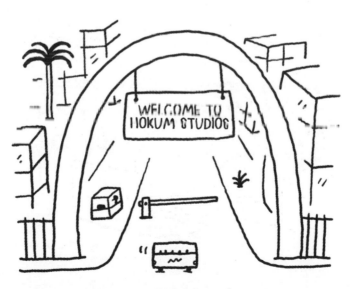

Hokum TV Studios

'Calm down now, kiddywinkles!'
cried Miss Spivak once we'd all been
marched into Hokum TV Studios.

'What's your amazekeel idea, Nance?' I whisper-shouted into Nancy's ear.

just your average boring old ear

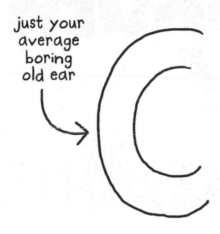

'Shhh! I'll tell you later,' whispered Nancy, as I spotted a man with a huge beard and tattoos all the way up his arms walking towards Miss Spivak. Both his earlobes had ring-holes in them big enough to poke a grown-up finger through.

'Atticus!' screamed Miss Spivak, giving the bearded baddy a big cuddle. 'Everyone, this is Atticus - he organised the trip for us today.'

now
that's
an ear

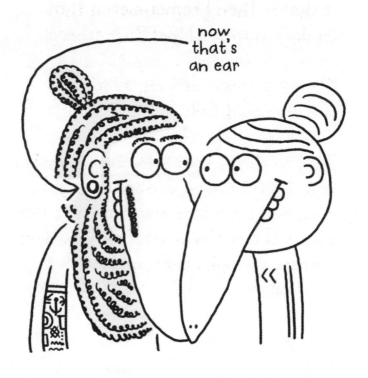

I leaned over to Bunky. 'Atticus?'
I whispered. 'What kind of a name
is that?' Then I remembered that
Bunky's name is Nigel Zuckerberg,
mine is Barry Loser and Nancy's is
Nancy Verkenwerken, so it's not
like we could talk.

'Ooh so this is your new fancy man
is it, Miss?' giggled Shazza. 'Very
nice. Bit hairy. Like the tats. Not sure
about the earlobe holoo though, you
can see straight through him!'

Miss Spivak's cheeks turned red like a traffic light and Sharonella stopped talking. Maybe she was waiting for them to go green so she could start nattering again.

Miss Spivak traffic lights

'How about we head off to the exhibition?' said Atticus, leading us to the lifts, which we all got into, and he pressed a button that took us down one floor.

The doors opened and we stepped out into a dark room with lit-up glass cabinets on either side. Atticus turned round and grinned.

look through these

'Welcome to the History of Television Exhibition!' he boomed, and we all did a groan.

The History of Television Exhibition

It was only ninety-nine seconds later and I was already boreder than a wild boar sniffing an ironing-board-sized cheeseboard displaying a selection of extremely bored-looking cardboard cut-out cheeses.

that

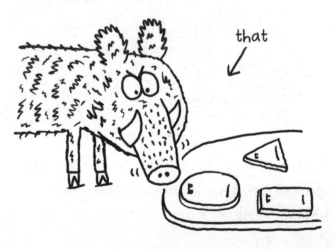

'On your right you will see a fine example of one of the first remote controls ever invented,' said Atticus, pointing at a wooden rectangle with a grey button on the front of it. It had a wire poking out of its bum which wound its way to the back of a black-and-white TV the size of a large washing machine.

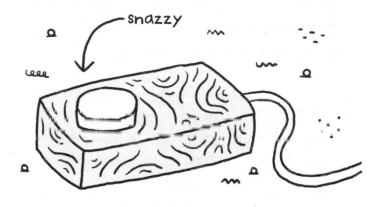

snazzy

'Fascinating,' said Nancy, lifting her glasses up and leaning in to get a better look.

My knees started to wobble with yawnosity. 'I wish I had a remote control that changed this boring old exhibition into a non-boring one,' I said, waiting to hear everyone laugh at my hilarikeel joke.

Nobody laughed.

I stretched my arm out and tapped
Nancy on the shoulder, thinking
how keel it'd be if I had a remote
control shoulder-tapper to save
me the hassle.

this is
not Nancy

'Psst, Nancy!' I whispered. 'About that
idea of yours . . .'

'And over here is our **Future Ratboy**
display,' said Atticus.

You know how I said my knees were beginning to wobble? Well now they snapped in half. I collapsed to the floor and peered up, seeing a whole glass cabinet filled with **Future Ratboy** stuff.

'B-by the power of keelness . . .' I stuttered, dragging my body across the zigzaggedy carpet towards the cabinet.

Atticus's mouth was opening and closing as if words were coming out of it, but nothing was going down my ears. All I could do was stare at the display.

FUTURE RATBOY
COSTUME

A fat little mannequin wearing a faded old Future Ratboy costume was standing tiltedly in the middle of the cabinet. Next to it, hanging on a dusty see-through plastic wire, was a scuffed-up cuddly Not Bird with one eye.

Not Bird, in case you didn't know, is **Future Ratboy's** sidekick. All he ever does is shout 'NOT!' after everything Ratboy says.

Signed photos of all the actors
from the TV show were sellotaped
onto the back wall of the display,
including one of a bald, podgy man
with a big bushy moustache.

Underneath the photo was a yellow
strip of paper with 'Rock Blondsky'
printed on it.

Bunky pressed his nose up to the glass and scrunched his face up like he needed to do a blowoff. 'Erm, excuse me Mr Atticus,' he said, 'but who in the name of unkeelness is Rock Blondsky?'

Who Rock Blondsky was

I stumbled to my feet and brushed myself down. Not with a brush though, with my hands.

Atticus's mouth started to open,
but it only got as wide as one of his
earlobe-holes.

identikeel

'Thank you Atticus,' I interrupted.
'I think I can take it from here.'

'Rock Blondsky,' I said, pointing at the photo of him, 'was none other than the first ever **Future Ratboy** actor.'

Every-
body
gasped.

'B-but there's only ever been one
Future Ratboy actor,' stuttered
Bunky. 'And that's Michael J Socks!'

'Oh yeah?' I said. 'Maybe you
shouldn't have forgotten to renew
your membership of the Future
Ratboy Fan Club, Nigel.'

I thought of my stack of **Future Ratboy** Fan Club magazines at home next to my bed and gave myself an upside-down, back-to-front salute for memorising every page of each one of them off by heart.

Bunky bowed his head in shame.

Atticus looked at Miss Spivak, who shrugged her shoulders. I don't think he was exackerly loving me taking over his tour, not that I cared.

'How come I've never seen this Rock Blondsky fella in any **Future Ratboy** episodes?' asked Darren, pulling a Cherry Fronkle out of his rucksack and cracking it open.

'They don't show his episodes any more,' I said.

'But why?' asked Bunky, and I leaned
forward and lowered the volume of
my voice until it was just a whisper.

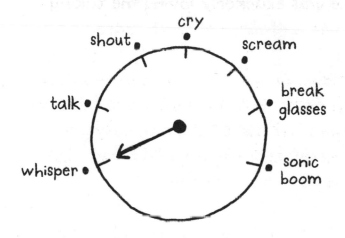

'Two words,' I said. 'The Curse
of Ratboy!'

The Curse of Ratboy

'That's four words,' said Nancy.

'Not if you don't count "of",' I said.
'And who in the name of unkeelness
counts "of"?'

'It's three words if you don't count "of",' said Nancy, but I just ignored her because what I had to say was far too important for that sort of nonsense.

'W-what IS this curse you speak of, Barry?' stuttered Bunky, looking scared.

The light from the display cabinet was casting his shadow against the wall beside him, and the silhouette of his nose looked absokeely ginormerloserous.

'It's what happened to Rock Blondsky after he stopped playing **Future Ratboy**,' I said all seriously.

I glanced over at Atticus, who was fiddling with his earlobe-hole, which I think might be what he does when he's annoyed someone knows more about something than him.

Atticus's ear

'Why DID he stop playing Future Ratboy?' asked Shazza.

'He got too old,' I said, pointing at the photo of him inside the glass cabinet. 'Note the moustache,' I smiled, sounding like the detective in my mum's favourite TV show, Detective Manksniff.

'Moustache . . . moustache . . . moustache . . .' echoed my voice inside my head. Something about that word was making a lightbulb flicker in my brain.

Darren fiddled with the ring pull on his Cherry Fronkle then looked up, his piggy little eyes all wide. 'So what happened to him after that then, Bazza?' he burped.

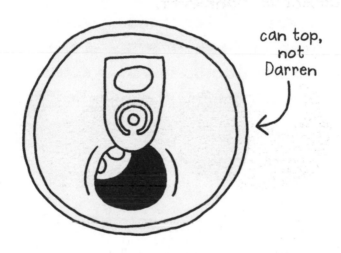

can top, not Darren

'Nobody wanted to hire him for any other TV shows,' I said. 'He was too well known as **Future Ratboy** - every time he auditioned for a part, all anyone could see was a half-rat, half-boy, half-TV.'

Gordon zoomed his eyes in on the photo of Rock Blondsky. 'He looks more like a half-sofa in that picture,' he chuckled.

'It's true,' I said. 'Once the curse struck, he started spending all his money on cheeseburgers - he couldn't be bothered to do anything except sit around at home watching repeats of his show.'

Nancy, who looked like she'd heard enough about Rock Blondsky, rolled her eyes. 'I thought you said they didn't show his episodes any more?' she said.

'Well remembered, Miss Verkenwerken,' I said, giving her a mini-salute. 'And they don't. After a few years, people stopped watching the re-runs. Everyone wanted new episodes.'

'So is that when Michael J Socks took over?' asked Bunky.

'Exactikeels!' I said. 'They came up with an all-new version of the show and Rock Blondsky was comperleeterly forgotten about. Nobody's seen him for years. Some say he roams the set of **Future Ratboy,** dressed up in an alien costume . . .'

'Anyhoos,' said Atticus, clapping his hands together and pointing to the next glass cabinet. 'Do you think we should move on?'

I looked at Atticus's hairy beard, then at Rock Blondsky's moustache, and the lightbulb in my brain turned from a flicker to a glow. 'Yes, good idea Atticus,' I grinned.

The hot dog plan

'Nancy!' I whispered, as Atticus led us to a display cabinet filled with loads of different-shaped TV aerials.

'You simperly HAVE to tell me your escape plan this exact billisecond!'

Nancy sighed. 'Two words,' she said. 'Food poisoning.'

'That's not two words,' I said, immedikeely realising it was:

1. food

2. poisoning

'What d'you mean, "food poisoning"?' I whisperered.

'Just pretend you've all got food poisoning,' said Nancy. 'That way you can go off to the toilets together.'

'Who's gonna believe we've ALL got food poisoning?' snuffled Darren as we shuffled on to another boring old display cabinet.

Nancy scrunched her face up, trying to listen to what Atticus was saying.

'I don't know, pretend the whole lot of you went round Bunky's for dinner last night and ate something disgusting,' she whispered out of the corner of her mouth.

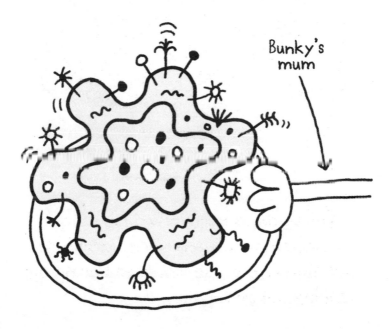

Bunky's mum

'I like it!' I said. 'Bunky, what did you have for din-dins last night?'

Bunky did his thinking-back-to-what-he-had-for-dinner-last-night face. 'Hot dogs!' he grinned.

get it?

'OK everyone, follow my lead,' I said, dropping back down onto my knees and getting ready to do some seriously amazekeel acting.

Best acting ever

'Urgh, I feel SICK!' I cried in my extra-loud voice. 'Bunky, I think it must be food poisoning from those hot dogs your mum served us when me and Nancy came round your house for dinner last night.'

I winked at Bunky and Nancy, and Nancy trod on my little finger. 'Oi,' she whispered. 'Don't include me in your stupid little plan - I want to stay here and see the exhibition!'

my little
finger
in better
times

Darren patted his forehead and
burped, doing a fake faint onto the
zigzaggedy carpet.

'Help me, I think I'm gonna poo
myself,' he cried. 'Curse Mrs
Zuckerberg's hot dogs - I wish
I hadn't accepted that invitation to
dinner round yours last night, Bunky!'

I twizzled my neck from where I was lying and peered across the carpet at Darren's sweaty head. 'Who said you could join in, Darrenofski?' I whisper-whispered. 'This plan is for me, Bunky and Nancy only!'

'Bleurgh, I feel a bit dodgy too!' gurgled Sharonella, sinking to her knees. 'I knew those frankfurters didn't look right. I think my bun was mouldy. And what was with the sauce - is ketchup sposed to be green?'

I tapped Bunky's shoe. 'Are you gonna get down here or what?' I whisper-shouted. 'I don't wanna sneak off with just these two losers!'

Bunky's knees started to wobble, and he collapsed onto the carpet next to me. 'Mamma, what have you done to us all?' he warbled.

Miss Spivak, who was standing behind Atticus, peered through his earlobe-holes at us all, lying like pieces of popcorn on a cinema carpet. 'What's wrong with you lot?' she asked.

'It was Bunky's mum's hot dogs,' I murmured, wondering if she'd been listening at all. 'Me, Bunky and Nancy ate seventeen trillion of them each last night and I think they might've been a bit off. Can we go to the toilets please?'

The Spivloser raised an eyebrow, looking like she was deciding whether to believe me or not. 'Go on then,' she sighed, and me and Bunky staggered off, Darren and Sharonella following behind.

'Nancy, are you coming too?' I said.

Miss Spivak looked at Nancy and nodded. 'I think that might be a good idea, Nancy,' she said, giving her a little nudge.

Walking towards a door

'Thanks a lot, Loser!' shouted Nancy, as we zoomed back up to the ground floor inside the lift. The doors opened and we all stepped out into the foyer.

'No problemo,' I smiled, peering around for a sign that pointed the way to the **Future Ratboy** set. 'Now, are you ready to hear what's been going on inside my ginormous brain?'

I spotted a door with a red lit-up sign saying 'ON AIR' above it and started walking towards it. Inside my head, the lightbulb was beginning to melt my ginormous child-genius brain.

'Remember when I was explaining about Rock Blondsky's moustache?' I asked, and they all nodded.

I pulled my magazine out of my rucksack and flipped to page twenty-one. 'It's happening to him too!' I said, pointing at Michael J Socks's mini moustache.

'But what's that got to do with anything?' said Shazza, looking all disappointed.

'It means Michael J Socks is getting too old to play Future Ratboy,' I smiled. 'Just like Rock Blondsky!'

We were still walking towards that door, by the way. It was taking way longer than I'd expected.

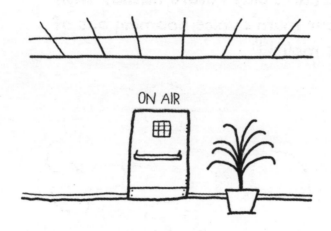

ON AIR

'I don't see the problem if Michael J Socks is growing a little 'tache,' snuffled Darren. 'He's pretending to be a RAT for crying out keel. Rats've got hair all over their bodies!'

'Ah ha, but he's pretending to be a rat-BOY, isn't he?' I said. 'Next thing you know his voice'll go deep. He can't play **Future Ratboy** with your mum's voice booming out of his mouth!'

DA7-7A!

'Eh?' said Darren, not exackerly getting my joke, which was this: Mrs Darrenofski's voice is really deep.

Shazza sniggled. 'Ha ha, your mum's voice IS well deep, Dazza!'

'No it's not!' said Darren, but you could tell he knew it was.

'Forget about Darren's mum's really deep voice,' I said, finally getting to the door. 'What I'm about to tell you is way more important . . .'

Future Rat-Bazzy

'You have GOT to be kidding me!' cackled Shazza, once I'd explained what I was thinking, which was this:

Michael J Socks was going to stop being the **Future Ratboy** actor soon because he was too old. Which meant somebody had to take over from him. And that somebody could be me.

'You don't actukeely think that could happen, do you Barry?' asked Bunky, holding in a sniggle.

'What's so blooming funny about it?' I cried, noticing something out of the corner of my eyeball.

A tall, thin security guard wearing sunglasses was standing on the other side of the foyer, staring across at us.

'So let me get this straight, Loser,' burped Darren. 'You reckon you're gonna be the next **Future Ratboy**?'

'I never said I was definitely going to take over,' I said. 'But they've got to replace Michael J Socks with SOMEBODY, haven't they? And I don't see why it shouldn't be me.'

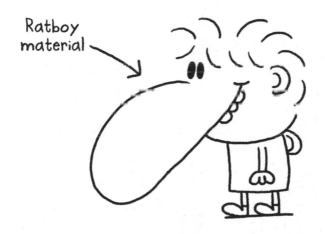

Ratboy material

'But what about the Curse of Ratboy?' asked Bunky. 'Aren't you scared?'

'That stupid curse doesn't bother me, Not Bird!' I boomed, doing my best **Future Ratboy** voice.

'Blimey Bazza, you'd better work on your Ratboy voice if you wanna get that part,' chuckled Sharonella.

Bunky took a deep breath. 'Nice try though, Loser!' he boomed in HIS **Future Ratboy** voice.

'Wowzoids, that was like Future Ratboy was actukeely here in the room with us!' said Shazza, clapping her hands. I looked up and saw the security guard's long legs striding towards us.

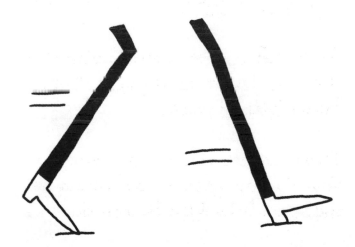

Darren smiled at me in an unsmiley way. 'Maybe you should audition to be Not Bird, Barry!' he cackled.

'Oh please,' I said. 'Everyone knows Bunky's MY sidekick. It just wouldn't work the other way round.'

Shazza shook her head. 'I dunno Bazzy,' she said. 'I've always thought of you as Bunky's sidekick to be honest.'

'Yeah well Shaz,' I said, trying to think of something really clever and funny to say back to her as I pushed the door open and stepped through, 'you're stupid.'

On the set

The door slammed behind us and I glanced around. We were standing in what looked like some kind of back alley. Except instead of proper walls, it had wooden boards with bricks painted on them.

'I–is this the **Future Ratboy** set?' gasped Bunky.

'Follow me, gang,' I said, running to the end of the fake road and turning left, zooming down a zigzaggedy maze of pretend passageways at super-loser speed.

'Wait for us!' cried Darren, the whole lot of them following behind me like I was their leader, which I am.

'There, that should've shaken off the security guard,' I smiled, skidding to a stop at the top of another fake street.

Nancy looked around. 'Erm, don't you think Miss Spivak is going to be wondering where we are?'

Sharonella pulled her rucksack straps tight and peered up at a fake wooden skyscraper disappearing off into the tangle of wires and spotlights hanging from the ceiling above. 'Don't worry about old Spivvy,' she smiled. 'She's far too busy peering into lover boy's earlobe-holes to worry about us.'

'Yeah, don't worry so much, Nancy!'
I grinned.

And that's when I heard the noise of
a lid sliding off a bin.

Spider fingers

'What in the name of unkeelness was that?' said Bunky, twizzling his head round.

'Relax, Not Bird,' I said, staring down the street and spotting a bin with its lid off. The whole thing was wobbling as if something was inside.

'Hey, what gives?' groaned a sleepy voice out of the bin. 'Some of us are trying to get some shut-eye over here!'

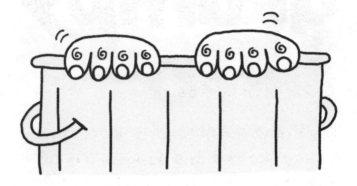

Eight filthy fingers crawled over the top of the bin like two fat spiders. Then a head popped up.

A head like no other head I'd ever seen before.

The grumpy alien

You know how I said I'd never seen a head like the one popping out of the bin before? That's because this one belonged to a ginormous, green, grumpy-looking alien.

'Waaahhh!!! Alien attack!' screamed Bunky, as I stared at the huge yellow nose poking out the front of its face.

Waggling out of the top of the alien's head, on four long wobbly sticks, were the same number of googly eyes, their pupils all pointing in comperleeterly different directions.

'Let's get the unkeelness out of here!' I wailed, blowing off with fear.

'Relax - it's only a costume!' said Sharonella, pointing at two tiny eye-slits deep inside the alien's mouth. 'So much for you two being superheroes!' she chuckled.

'Hmm, an alien costume,' muttered Nancy. 'Where have I heard someone mention that before?'

Deep inside my massive child-genius brain, a tiny little bell started to ring. But before I had time to think about it, the alien heaved itself out of the bin.

It brushed itself down with its great big rubbery green frog hands and scratched its head. 'Eurgh, what time is it?' it boomed in a deep, growly voice.

Nancy looked at her watch. 'Twelve thirty-eight,' she said.

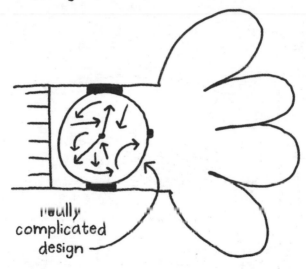

really complicated design

'Argh! I'll be late for my scene with Michael J Socks!' roared the alien. 'Thanks for the wake up call, kiddos!'

Darren gasped, then burped. 'He must be one of the actors from the **Future Ratboy** show!' he grinned.

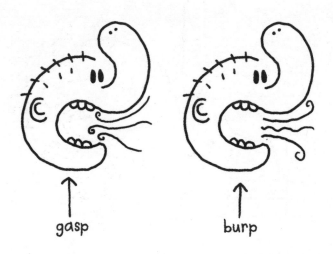

gasp   burp

Nancy ignored Darren. 'Who in the keelness climbs inside a BIN for a nap though?' she said.

'I'm with Nance,' said Shazza. 'A grown man snoozing inside a smelly old bin? It just ain't right!'

The alien twizzled round to face Shazza, its huge yellow nose boinging up and down. 'Who you calling a MAN?' it bellowed. 'My name's Sheila. Sheila Taramasalata.'

This time we all gasped, not because the alien was a lady, but because her second name was so RIDONKEELOUS.

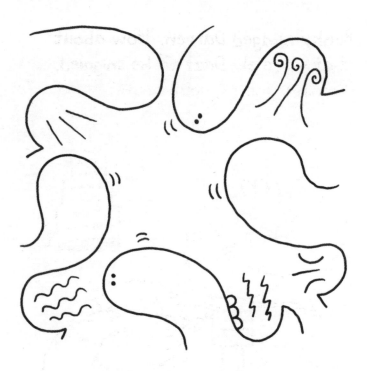

'Ever so sorry, Mrs Taramasalata!' sniggled Shazza.

'Yeah well,' grumbled Sheila. 'You remember that name - I'm gonna be famous one of these days!'

Bunky nudged Darren. 'How about that voice eh, Dazza?' he sniggled. 'Reminds me of your mum!'

'Shut up, Bunky!' snapped Darren, as I suddenly realised something - Sheila Taramasalata would know the way to the **Future Ratboy** set!

'Erm, excuse me Sheila,' I said, stepping forward and putting my hand up like I was at school. 'But you wouldn't be able to point us towards Michael J Socks, would you?'

Monsieur Tummy

Sheila scratched her rubbery head. 'Hmm, now let me think,' she mumbled. 'Guess I oughta know, seeing as I'm sposed to be acting opposite him right about now!'

At the end of the fake street
were two alleyways going off in
comperleeterly opposite directions.
'It's defo one of these two ways,' she
said. 'Trouble is, kiddos - which one?'

Behind us I heard the sound of footsteps. There was quite a long gap between each one of them, and I guessed it must be that security guard with the really long legs running down the passageways to catch us.

I stared at the two alleyways facing us and imagined I was standing in front of my fridge at home, deciding what to eat. 'Quick, tell me what to do, Monsieur Tummy,' I whispered, and my belly started to grumble.

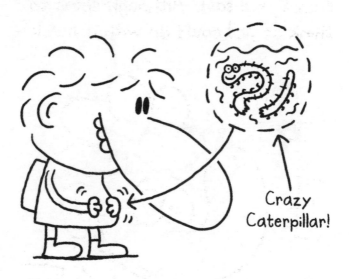

Crazy Caterpillar!

'What in the name of unkeelness are you doing, Loser?' asked Shazza.

'I always ask Monsieur Tummy when I'm working out what to eat,' I said. 'He never gets it wrong.'

Shazza crumpled her face up like a piece of paper with a rubbish drawing on it. 'But we aren't choosing food, Bazza,' she said. 'Although come to think of it, I could do with a snack.'

Madame Tummy

'Shhh!' I shushed, closing my eyes
and letting my belly do his business.
'Monsieur Tummy is trying to think.'

Sheila Taramasalata pointed at me
over her shoulder with her thumb.
'He's a funny little one, isn't he?' she
said, and I was just about to say
something back to her when
Monsieur Tummy interrupted.

My way or the other way

'Silence, for Monsieur Tummy has spoken!' I boomed, as the sound of footsteps got louder. I pointed at the passageway leading to the left. 'This is the way to the Future Ratboy set.'

'Hmmm,' hmmed Sheila, peering through her eye-slits to the right. 'No offence to Mr Stomach down there, buddy, but I'd have to say the complete opposite.'

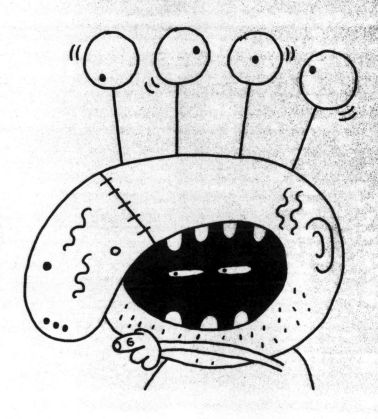

Shazza looked at my belly, then up at Sheila Taramasalata inside her stupid costume. 'I'm with her,' she said, pointing at the four googly eyes waggling out the top of the rubbery alien mask.

Darren sidled over to Sharonella. 'Me too,' he burped.

Nancy pushed her glasses up her nose and tiptoed next to Shaz and Daz. 'Sorry Barry,' she said.

'It's Monsieur Tummy you should be apologising to, Nancy,' I said, turning to Bunky. 'Right, come on Not Bird, let's go meet Michael J Socks before that security guard catches us.'

Bunky smiled at me the way my dad did that time one of his blowoffs accidentally kickstarted the domino rally I'd been setting up for three hours.

PARP!

'Soz Baz,' he said, nodding down at my belly. 'It's just . . . this whole Mr Tummy thing's a bit too weird - even for me.'

'It's MONSIEUR Tummy,' I boomed. 'And as the official leader of this group, I say we go MY way!'

Sheila Taramasalata lifted one of her flip-floppy frog feet and plonked it back down, half a metre further in the direction she'd decided.

I stared at my soon-to-be-ex-friends
and growled as a long leg appeared
round the corner at the top of the
fake street.

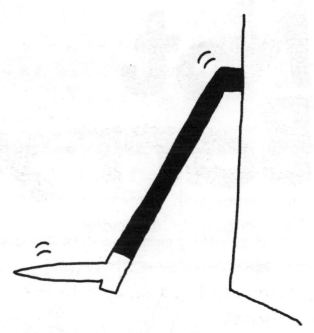

'If any one of you lot move even
half a trillimetre towards that
passageway, I will never speak to
you ever again!' I whisper-growled.

Not Barry

'Wait for me!' I cried eight billiseconds later, running down the wrong passageway to catch up with my ex-friends.

'I thought you were never gonna speak to any of us again?' giggled Darren, jiggling his bum as he followed the flailing green tail sticking out of Sheila Taramasalata's stupid rubber alien costume.

'Not far now, I can almost smell it!'
said Sheila, turning left, then left
again, then right, then going straight
on for a bit.

'This is SO comperleeterly the wrong
way, Bunky!' I cried. 'Come on, please
let's go back!'

Sharonella twizzled her head round like an owl wearing plastic earrings. 'Thought you said Bunky was YOUR sidekick, Loser,' she sniggled. 'Doesn't sound like that to me!'

owl

Shaz

'Yeah Barry,' chuckled Bunky in his Future Ratboy voice. 'Or should I call you . . . Not Bird?'

Sheila Taramasalata pointed over her shoulder at Bunky. 'Now THAT'S a good **Future Ratboy** impression,' she growled.

My nose drooped, tilting my head down with it, and I peered at Sheila's alien feet. 'Nancy's right about that costume of yours,' I said. 'It really does ring a bell.'

MINI CLANG

'Oh yeah?' said Sheila, carrying on walking.

'Weird you haven't taken your mask off,' I said. 'You must be hot in there.'

'Oh, I'm alright,' said Sheila. 'This thing's far too big to carry under your arm - may as well leave it on your head,' she chuckled.

'Bit like Barry's nose!' cackled Sharonella, like hers is any smaller than mine.

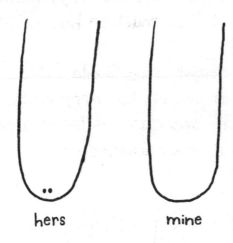

hers   mine

We walked through a door at the end of the passageway and out into another TV set. 'That's right,' I said. 'You all have a good laugh while you comperleeterly ruin my day.'

Grannies every-where

'Hey, I know this place!' cried Sharonella. 'It's the Detective Manksniff set.'

'Oh yeah!' said Bunky. 'This is my mum's favourite show.'

'Mine too,' I said, looking around. Sharonella was right - we were standing in the back garden of Detective Manksniff's TV house.

Detective Manksniff, in case you didn't know, is a show about a detective called Detective Manksniff who solves a different crime every week.

always chewing on a straw

All the mums and grannies in Mogden comperleeterly fancy him.

'Ladies, ladies, ladies,' boomed a skinny old man in a white suit and hat. 'Welcome to the set of Detective Manksniff!'

I twizzled my head and spotted
a gaggle of curly white-haired
grannies, all wearing identikeel light
blue polyester jackets.

From a distance they looked like
fluffy clouds moving slowly across
the sky.

'My gran would love this!' said
Sharonella, and I rewound my brain
to the time I went round her house
and found out she lived with
her granny.

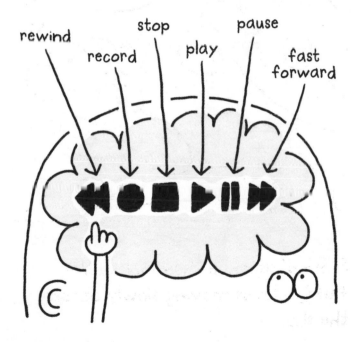

The eight million old ladies circled round Detective Manksniff's fake swimming pool like a necklace of blueberry-flavour marshmallows, taking photos and nattering about how dishy he was.

'Right, that's enough of this,' I said. 'Let's go find the **Ratboy** set.'

man of action

Bunky patted me on the head. 'Relax, Not Bird!' he said in his **Future Ratboy** voice. 'There's plenty of time to find Michael J Socks.'

'Besides,' said Shazza, patting her tummy and pointing over at a table full of tiny little triangle-shaped sandwiches. 'Looks like lunch is served!'

Egg cress sarnies

It was three hundred and seventy six seconds later and I was sitting at a fold-up table, squidged between two old grannies called Zelda and Dot.

'Do you think they'll mind us budging in like this?' said Nancy, who was sitting on the other side of Dot.

'Just wrinkle your face up like an oldie and keep scoffing,' said Sharonella's voice, which was coming from the other side of Zelda.

'Ooh, you can't beat a nice egg cress sandwich, can you Dot?' warbled Zelda. Dot nodded, biting down on her sarnie like a creased-up old newt wearing false teeth.

I peeled my tiny triangle of bread open and peered inside. 'Why do they even bother making this stuff?' I said, pointing at the tiny leaves of cress. 'All it's ever used for is egg sandwiches. And who in the keelness eats them?'

me if I was
a mm tall

'You, by the looks of it,' said Sheila Taramasalata, who was sitting opposite me, still inside her alien costume. She slotted an eggy triangle into the hole underneath her yellow rubber nose and a chomping sound echoed around inside her mask.

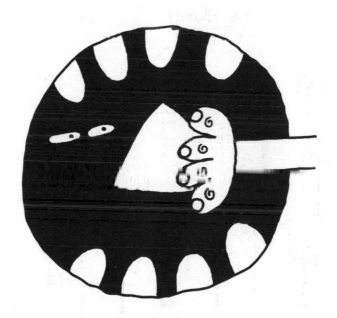

Darren piled three sandwiches on top of each other and squished them down to the height of one.

'Why don't you just relax and enjoy yourself for once, Not Bird?' he snarfled, swallowing the whole thing down like a hippo.

'Enjoy myself?' I said, taking a bite.
'This was supposed to be my big day.
I was gonna meet Michael J Socks!'

SHARK!!!

'Now look at me - eating an egg
cress sandwich in the middle of
a giant blueberry marshmallow
necklace.'

Bunky and Nancy glanced at each other, like a mum and dad worrying whether their kid had gone bonkoids.

Sharonella snaffled a sandwich and sniggled, bits of egg and cress leaves flying out of her mouth like chunks of exploding planet. 'I've said it before and I'll say it again, Bazza,' she chuckled. 'You do make me LARF!'

'Nancy, you're a sensible young lady,'
I said, sounding like one of the
grannies. A tiny little full-stop-sized
globule of egg flew out of my
mouth-hole and landed on her
lip. 'Surely you'd rather be on the
Future Ratboy set than . . .'
I waggled my hand around at the
old grannies. 'HERE?!'

massively
clouding
my day

Nancy dabbed at her lip with a napkin and thought for a millisecond. "I'd rather be in the History of Television Exhibition, actukeely," she said. "But a certain somebody had other ideas, didn't they?"

who could it be?

'I think she means you, Not Bird!'
laughed Bunky, biting down on his
soggy triangle like he thought he was
Future Ratboy.

'Would you PERLEASE stop calling
me Not Bird,' I said, standing up and
looking around for a toilet.

I don't know if it was Monsieur
Tummy worrying about his owner
missing out on seeing Michael J Socks,
or the five egg and cress sandwiches
I'd just swallowed, but I suddenly
really needed a poo.

'Yeurgh, who blew off?'

shouted Darren, and I fake-pinched my nostrils.

'Zelda! Was that you?' I said, spotting a line of old grannies queuing up in front of a door, and I waddled off in their direction.

Counting blueberry marsh- mallows

I joined the queue of identikeel old grannies at the back, immedi-speed-counting how many of them there were in front of me.

Once I'd done that, I timesed the number by five, which is how many minutes I guessed each one of them would take inside the cubicle.

'Three hundred and twelvety-eight minutes?' I mumbled to myself. 'I can't hold this thing in that long!'

The old woman in front of me twizzled round at one millimetre per minute. 'What's that you say, dear?' she cooed.

twizzling

'Oh nothing,' I sighed. 'It's just - I was sposed to be meeting Michael J Socks you see, and now I'm standing here behind seven trillion blueberry marshmallows trying not to let an egg cress sandwich push a poo out of my bum.'

The granny looked down at me like a granny worrying her grandson had gone bonkoids.

And that's when an egg-shaped bubble of blowoff popped out of my bum.

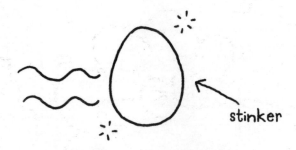

stinker

'Oh my good gracious me,' shrieked the granny, whipping a hanky out of her sleeve and holding it up to her saggy nostrils. 'I think I'm going to faint!'

'Granny down!' I cried, looking around for the old man in the white suit and hat. 'We've got a granny going down over here!'

But it was too late - she'd already started to topple.

Domino grannies

'Tell my kitty I love him!' wailed the old granny as she fell backwards, knocking into the identikeel old lady in front of her in the queue.

Kitty

'Ooh, crumpets!' shouted that granny, toppling into the next one in line.

'Argh, me hip!' cried that one, waggling her arms in the air like a whisk as she fell forwards into another blueberry marshmallow.

I stood back and started to whistle, pretending not to notice as the whole line of them started to drop, all the way up to the toilet door.

Big trouble for little Bazzy

If there's one thing I learnt that day in Hokum TV Studios, it's this: there's nothing like setting off a domino rally of old grannies to stop you needing a poo.

'Ooh blimey, I'm late for my scene,' said Sheila Taramasalata, wiping her fake rubber lips with a napkin and starting to head back the way we'd come.

The queue of grannies lay sprawled on the floor, rolling around on their light blue polyester backs like turtles after a hurricane.

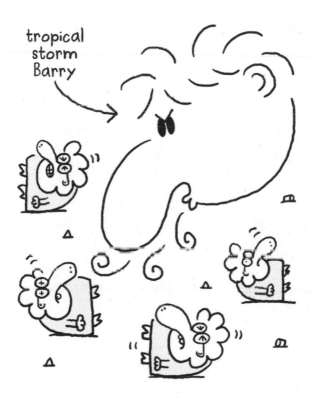

tropical storm Barry

'Michael J Socks here we come!' said Bunky, grabbing me by the hood on my jumper. 'Come on Not Bird, let's get the keelness out of here before you cause any more trouble.'

NOBODY touches my hood

'If you call me Not Bird one more time . . .' I cried, trying to work out what I was going to say I'd do if Bunky called me Not Bird one more time.

I peered around for an idea, and immedikeely spotted a familikeels-looking security guard barging his way through the crowd of cooing grannies, right towards us.

'There you are ya little punk!' he panted, grabbing my hood out of Bunky's hand and whipping a walkie-talkie out of his belt. 'Loser located,' he shouted into it. 'Repeat: Loser located!'

'How did you know my name?'
I said, trying to run off, but my
hood wouldn't let me.

I don't know why they have to sew
hoods onto jumpers so well. They
should just be stuck on with velcro so
you can rip them off like a lizard's
tail or something.

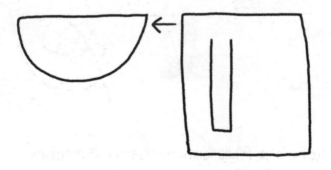

The security guard pulled his
sunglasses off his face and peered
down at me with angry cross-eyes.
Which I could have said were cross
cross-eyes, but I thought that might
be a bit confusing.

'There's a Miss Spivak been searchin'
for you lot,' he snarled.

'I told you she'd be looking for us!' shouted Nancy.

'Why don't you take your hands off Not Bird, you big bully!' cried Sharonella, stomping on the security guard's foot, and he screamed, letting go of my hood.

I looked at Bunky, then Darren, then Sharonella, then Nancy, then Sheila Taramasalata inside her stupid costume.

'Run for it!'

I boomed.

Not running for it at all

If there's another thing I learnt that day, it's this: sometimes when you shout 'Run for it!', nobody runs.

'Nah,' said Darren, finishing off a corner of sandwich and doing an eggy burp in Sharonella's face.
'I'm all full up.'

'Me too,' said Sharonella, blowing Darren's burp in the direction of Zelda. 'Let's just go back to the History of Television Exhibition and have a nice snooze shall we?'

looks exackerly like Dot

'WHAT?!' I cried, looking at Bunky. 'Ratboy,' I said, trying to get him to do what I wanted. 'You still want to see Michael J Socks, don't you?'

Bunky's mouth opened to the width of one of Sheila Taramasalata's eye-slits, but before it could get any bigger, the tall, thin little security guard had interrupted.

eye-slit

mouth

'Roger that,' he shouted into his walkie-talkie. Then he looked up and said the keelest twelve words I've ever heard:

'Looks like you little ratbags are off to the **Future Ratboy** set.'

Future Ratgirl

'Here they are, Miss Spivak,' said the security guard, as we trundled onto the set of **Future Ratboy**.

Miss Spivak twizzled round and glared down at us all. Behind her stood Atticus and the rest of my loserish class, futuristikeel fake buildings towering up to the ceiling lights in the background.

'Where in the name of Mogden have you lot been?' she screeched.

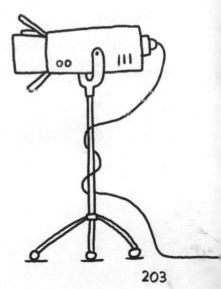

I stared up at her, my mouth hanging open. 'What are YOU doing here?' I gasped.

Gordon Smugly stepped forward. 'Should've stuck around, Loser,' he smiled. 'You missed the best bit of the day!'

I stared at Gordon, trying to work out why he looked so different. Then I realised what it was. He was wearing a green rubber alien outfit, exackerly the same as Sheila Taramasalata's.

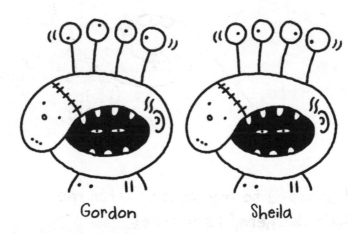

Gordon   Sheila

Stuart Shmendrix grinned. 'Yeah Barry, cos after the History of Television Exhibition bit finished, we all came here to the **Future Ratboy** set and met Michael J Socks!'

I dropped to my knees. 'T-tell me he's still here,' I stuttered.

'Too late, Losoid,' sneered Gordon.
'But you would've loved him.
Wouldn't he, Fay?'

Fay Snoggles sniggled, looking all
excited about something. 'What are
you laughing about, Snoggles?' I said,
and she looked down at her feet.

'Oh, nothing much,' she said.

'Nothing much?' boomed Atticus. 'Don't be so modest, Fay!' He turned to me, his floppy earlobes waggling. 'Mr Socks was very impressed with Fay's acting.'

'Acting?' I said. 'What are you talking about, "acting"?'

Atticus smiled. 'I arranged for the class to be extras in the background of a scene,' he said.

'We're gonna be in a **Future Ratboy** episode!' squealed Stuart Shmendrix.

Miss Spivak put her hand on Fay's shoulder. 'And Michael thought this one here would make a great Future Ratgirl one day, didn't he, Fay?'

Fay's lips turned up as mine turned down.

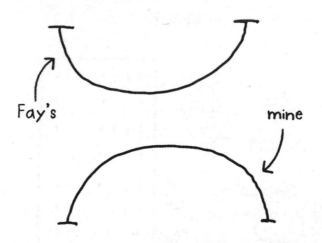

'But . . . but . . . but that was sposed to be meee!!!' I wailed, as Sheila Taramasalata stepped forward.

'Hey, what's this kid doing inside my spare costume?' she said, pointing at Gordon.

A lady with a clipboard stepped out from behind one of the fake wooden skyscrapers. 'There you are, Taramasalata,' she snapped. 'Where've you been?'

Sheila itched her rubbery bum.
'Oh, er, well I kinda bumped into these
little troublemakers, and then they
led me the wrong way, and well, you
know how these things go . . .'

Clipboard lady rolled her eyes.
'Always an excuse, isn't there,
Taramasalata,' she said.
'You're FIRED!'

Sheila dropped to her knees, just next to me. 'Nooo!!!' she whimpered. 'The Curse of Ratboy - it's struck again!'

'This is the worst school trip ever!' I cried, joining in with Sheila, and I was just about to give up comperleeterly on the whole day when that bell from earlier started ringing inside my brain again.

The great Blondsky reveal

'Hang on a millikeels,' I said, staggering to my feet and pointing at Sheila Taramasalata. She stopped crying and looked at me through her eye-slits. 'I knew there was something familikeels about that costume.'

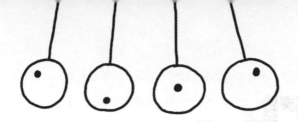

'What costume?' said Sheila, then she
realised I was talking about the alien
costume she was inside.

'Bunky,' I said, clicking my fingers.

'That's Ratboy to you, Not Bird!'
said Bunky.

'OK, Ratboy,' I said, because I didn't
have time to waste. 'Remember what
I said about Rock Blondsky earlier?'

Bunky tried to think, which is quite
hard for him. 'Nope,' he said.

Nancy whipped her glasses off.
'The alien costume!' she gasped.
'You said Rock Blondsky roamed the
Future Ratboy set dressed up in an
alien costume!'

I pointed at Nancy. 'Ten points to
the girl in the specs,' I said.

Atticus leaned over to Miss Spivak
and whispered something, and
she laughed.

Like I said earlier, I don't think he likes
it when there's someone who knows
more than him.

I twizzled round on the spot,
keeping my arm stretched out
until my finger was pointing in Sheila
Taramasalata's rubbery alien face.

'I knew your name was too weird to
be true,' I said, sounding like Detective
Manksniff. 'And the fact we found
you asleep in the bin - I should've
guessed there was something fishy
about that right away . . . or should
I say, something Future-Ratboy-y!'

The clipboard lady, who was still standing there, rolled her eyes, this time in the opposite direction.

'Asleep in a bin again eh, Taramasalata?' she said. 'You are DEFINITELY fired!'

'Not Bird, what in the name of unkeelness are you talking about?' said Bunky, and I reached up and patted him on the head the way you do to someone whose brain isn't big enough to understand.

'Prepare yourselves for a shock,
ladies and gentlekeels,' I said, stepping
towards the person who'd been
saying their name was Sheila
Taramasalata the whole afternoon.

I reached out, grabbed the side of the
rubbery alien mask and got ready to
whip it off. 'May I present to you the
original Future Ratboy actor - none
other than . . .

Rock Blondsky!

The bus back to Mogden

'How was I sposed to know it wasn't Rock Blondsky inside the costume?' I said, nine hundred and ninety eight seconds later.

I was sitting in the front row of the bus next to Sharonella, Nancy, Bunky and Darren so that Miss Spivak could keep an eye on us on the journey back to Mogden.

eyes in
back of
head

'At least the clipboard lady gave Sheila her job back,' said Nancy.

Sharonella nodded. 'Nice of Atticus to have a word with her, wasn't it?' she said. 'You've got a good one there, Miss Spivak. Still, shame about those earlobes innit.'

'You alright down there, losers?'
chuckled Gordon Smugly, who was
sitting on the back seat with Fay
Snoggles and Stuart Shmendrix,
thinking they were keel just because
they got to meet Michael J Socks
and be in a **Future Ratboy** episode.

feeling
queasy

'You've got to admit though,'
I said, rewinding my brain back
to the millisecond I ripped Sheila
Taramasalata's mask off and saw
her sweaty, non-Blondskoid face
underneath. 'She's got a ridikeelously
deep voice for a lady.'

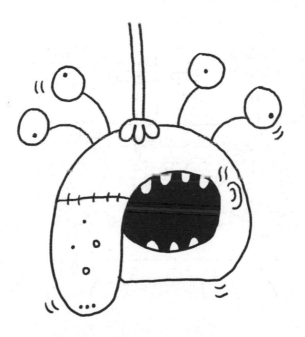

Darren peered out of the window as the skyscrapers of Hokum City got shorter and shorter in the distance. 'I never did get to try a Passion Fruit Fronkle,' he muttered, doing an eggy burp and blowing it in Bunky's face.

'Eurgh, I don't feel so good,' said Bunky.

'Me neither,' mumbled Nancy, who'd gone comperleeterly white.

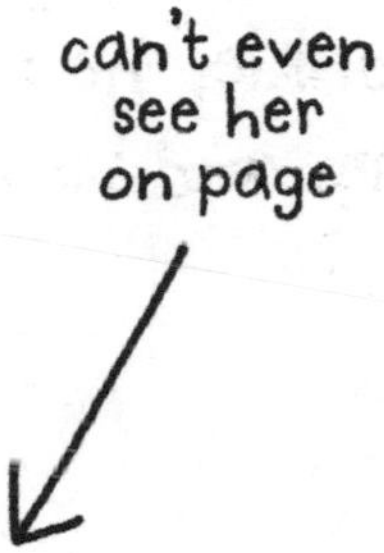
can't even
see her
on page

Miss Spivak twizzled round and smiled. 'I forgot to ask, did you lot manage to have any lunch?'

'Egg cress sarnies,' said Sharonella, a bead of sweat zigzagging down her forehead. 'Millions and millions of egg cress sarnies . . .'

The bus lurched round a corner then straightened up and bounced over a speed bump. 'Bleurgh,' I said, scrabbling around in my rucksack.

I whipped out the first thing my hand grabbed, which was my **Future Ratboy** Fan Club Magazine, and it flipped open to page twenty-one. Michael J Socks smiled out of the photo at me, and I stared back, my nose shrivelling up like a cold, mouldy cucumber.

won't be smiling in a second

'Definitely the worst school trip ever,' I said, getting ready to puke straight into his face.

Wat Boy and Not Birdy

'You just lie there on the sofa and take it easy, Barry,' said my mum.

I don't know how many seconds later it was, but somehow I'd managed to stumble home from school after the bus dropped us there.

'Sorry your big day didn't work out for you, love,' warbled my mum from the kitchen as Desmond toddled into the lounge holding a piece of paper.

excited to
see me

'Eurgh, you're the last thing I need,' I said, turning over and pressing my nose into the cushion.

A tiny little finger tapped my hand and I sighed. 'What is it, Des?' I groaned. 'Can't you see I've had a bad day?'

'Me done a drawing,' he said.

'Very good, Des,' I said. 'I'll see you later, OK?'

'Bazzy Wat Boy!' he said. 'Me Not Birdy!'

I rolled over and peered through my eye-slits at a blurry bit of paper with some scribbles on it. 'What's that?' I said.

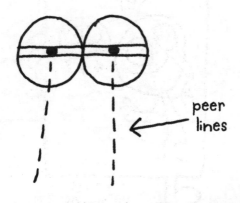

peer lines

Des pointed at the blue squiggle
on the left. 'Dat Bazzy Wat Boy!'
he smiled.

Then he pointed at a smaller, brown
squiggle on the right. 'Me Not Birdy!'

I opened my eyes to the size of Atticus's earlobe-holes and looked again. 'Wait a millikeels,' I said, pointing at the blue squiggle. 'Is that me as Future Ratboy?'

Des nodded.

I pointed at the brown squiggle. 'And that's you as Not Bird?' I chuckled.

'Yep,' smiled Des, proudly.

'Hmm, that's actukeely not bad,'
I said, smacking my lips. I was feeling
pretty thirsty after all that puking.

'Are you thirsty?' shouted my mum
from the kitchen. I think she must
have heard my lips smacking together.

super
mum
hearing

'I picked you up some Fronkle from
Feeko's this morning . . .

... new flavour – Passion Fruit!
Snazzy, eh?'

A tiny little cress-sized bubble of
excitement started to zigzag up from
my belly to my brain, and I smiled at
Des. 'Erm, Not Bird?' I said.

'Yeah?' smiled Des.

'Not Bird, do you think you could get
me a Passion Fruit Fronkle from
the fridge?'

'Yep,' said Desmond, waddling off
to the kitchen.

A key rattled in the door and my
dad walked into the hallway,
wiping his feet on the mat. 'Oo-ooh,
I'm ho-ome!' he called. 'How was my
big boy's big day?'

frazzled
from
work

I slumped into the sofa and chuckled to myself, thinking of everything that'd happened since he'd kissed my nose goodbye that morning.

'Not too bad I spose,' I said, the smell of sick and egg cress sandwiches wafting up my nostrils.